For Yannik

OTHER BOOKS BY MARCUS PFISTER

The Rainbow Fish *
Rainbow Fish to the Rescue! *
The Christmas Star *
Penguin Pete *
Penguin Pete's New Friends *
Penguin Pete and Pat
Penguin Pete, Ahoy!
Penguin Pete and Little Tim
Hopper *
Hopper Hunts for Spring
Hopper's Easter Surprise
Hang On, Hopper!

*Also available in Spanish

Copyright © 1996 by Nord-Süd Verlag AG, Gossau Zürich, Switzerland
First published in Switzerland under the title *Lieber Nikolaus wach auf!*
English translation copyright © 1996 by North-South Books Inc.

First published in the United States, Great Britain, Canada,
Australia, and New Zealand in 1996 by North-South Books,
an imprint of Nord-Süd Verlag AG, Gossau Zürich, Switzerland.

Distributed in the United States by North-South Books Inc., New York.

Library of Congress Cataloging-in-Publication Data is available.
A CIP catalogue record for this book is available from The British Library.
ISBN 1-55858-605-9 (trade binding)
1 3 5 7 9 TB 10 8 6 4 2
ISBN 1-55858-606-7 (library binding)
1 3 5 7 9 LB 10 8 6 4 2
Printed in Belgium

For more information about our books,
and the authors and artists who create them, visit our web site:
http://www.northsouth.com

Wake Up, Santa Claus!

Marcus Pfister

Translated by J. Alison James

North-South Books

New York / London

ONE WINTER DAY, the forest lay peacefully sleeping under a thick blanket of snow. An old wooden house stood in a small clearing. Nothing stirred, but the contented sound of snoring drifted outside. Someone was asleep, nestled deep in the warm feather bed. Only the lump under the covers and the tip of his nightcap showed that he was there.

It was Santa Claus. Slowly he turned and poked his nose above the covers. He blinked and yawned, and glanced at the clock on his little bedside table. Then he sat up with a start.

How could he have slept through the alarm clock, on today of all days? He'd really have to rush to deliver the children's presents on time. He jumped out of bed and ran to find his clothes.

Trousers, jacket, hat — where was his hat? On his head, of course. Now for his boots. He found one under the bed. Good. But where was the other? On top of the cupboard? Behind the door? In the chest? He looked under the bed again. The boot had vanished. At last he saw the shiny black toe peeking out from under the curtain.

"There you are!" he said to the boot. "Stop laughing at me. I'm late!" And he ran for the door.

But when he pulled it open, he was trapped by a wall of snow as high as his chin.

With a groan, he picked up his shovel and dug his way
through the heavy snow. Slowly he cleared a path across the
garden, though the gate, and out to the stable.

He leaned against the door to catch his breath. "Phew, I've
done it," he said thankfully.

But it had taken hours—hours that he didn't have.

Trousers, jacket, hat — where was his hat? On his head, of course. Now for his boots. He found one under the bed. Good. But where was the other? On top of the cupboard? Behind the door? In the chest? He looked under the bed again. The boot had vanished. At last he saw the shiny black toe peeking out from under the curtain.

"There you are!" he said to the boot. "Stop laughing at me. I'm late!" And he ran for the door.

But when he pulled it open, he was trapped by a wall of snow as high as his chin.

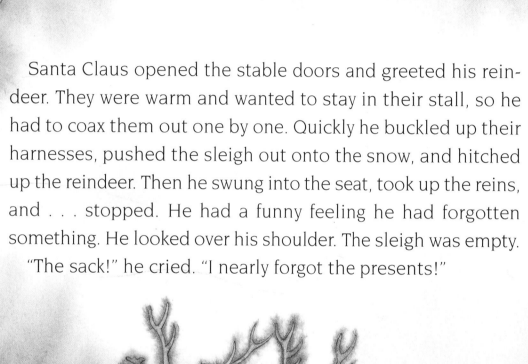

Santa Claus opened the stable doors and greeted his reindeer. They were warm and wanted to stay in their stall, so he had to coax them out one by one. Quickly he buckled up their harnesses, pushed the sleigh out onto the snow, and hitched up the reindeer. Then he swung into the seat, took up the reins, and . . . stopped. He had a funny feeling he had forgotten something. He looked over his shoulder. The sleigh was empty.

"The sack!" he cried. "I nearly forgot the presents!"

He ran back into the house and found the sack leaning against the fireplace in his living room. Santa dragged it over to the door, but no matter how he pushed and shoved and dragged and tugged, the sack wouldn't fit through the door. There was nothing else to do: He would have to put all the presents into smaller sacks.

He raced to the cellar and found three sacks. Then he began to unpack all the presents. Apples, nuts, and oranges rolled all over the floor. Santa Claus had to scramble to gather them up and stuff them in the sacks. Finally he was finished. Out of breath, he loaded the sacks into the sleigh, and jumped up on his seat.

"Ready at last, my friends. Off we go!"

But the reindeer wouldn't budge. They stamped their feet and snorted.

"Oh, of course, what was I thinking?" said Santa Claus. "I was in such a hurry, I forgot to feed you! How could you ever go such a distance on empty stomachs?" Quickly he brought out two big bales of hay and two buckets of water. Slowly and steadily the reindeer began to eat.

It was getting cold, and more snow was beginning to fall. Santa Claus hopped impatiently from foot to foot.

Finally the reindeer had eaten their fill. For the third time, Santa Claus climbed up on his sleigh. "Heigh ho, off we go!" he cried.

The reindeer pulled with all their might. They leaned into the harness and strained with their legs, but the sleigh seemed to be stuck to the ground.

Suddenly it moved forward with a jerk, slipped a few feet, then stuck again.

Santa Claus got down and wiped the snow from the runners. The fine smooth blades that he kept polished so carefully all year were suddenly cracked and covered with rust! No wonder the sleigh was stuck.

Santa Claus was close to tears. "What a nightmare!" he cried. "We'll never make it, even if I push." But push he did, and when that didn't work, he pulled. The snow fell faster and thicker, and soon he couldn't even see the sleigh. He knew the reindeer were struggling with him; he felt their warm breath. But when the track disappeared in the blowing snow, he had no idea where to go.

Sick at heart, he followed the harness back to the sleigh and climbed in. The reindeer couldn't move forwards or backwards. They were stuck, chest deep in the heavy snow.

It was hopeless.

Then from off in the distance, he heard the soft ringing of bells. The sound grew nearer and nearer, louder and louder, until . . .

Santa Claus woke up!

He sat up and turned off the alarm clock. Was it really only a dream? He hopped out of bed and quickly got dressed. His two boots stood neatly under the chair, just where he had left them. Cautiously he opened the door to look outside. The path to the stable was clear of snow. He ran out to check on the reindeer. They were happily eating hay from their mangers. And the runners on the sleigh were polished like mirrors.

Santa Claus jumped for joy.

He ran back to the house.

The presents were stuffed in the sack, but it wasn't too big to fit through the doorway. He loaded it into the sleigh and harnessed up the reindeer.

Without a backwards glance, Santa Claus shouted, "Heigh ho, off we go!" and the sleigh slipped like a snowflake across the open trail. Then with a surge of speed, the reindeer bounded into the air, and the sleigh rose gently up and up, and disappeared into the cold moonlit sky.

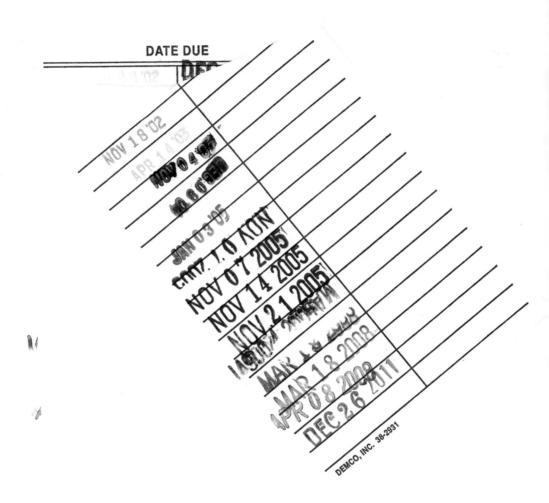